D1622031

FAQ

TEEN LIFE™

FREQUENTLY ASKED QUESTIONS ABOUT

Drug Testing

Jonas
Pomere

ROSEN
PUBLISHING®

New York

Published in 2007 by The Rosen Publishing Group, Inc.
29 East 21st Street, New York, NY 10010

Library of Congress Cataloging-in-Publication Data

Pomere, Jonas.
Frequently asked questions about drug testing / Jonas Pomere. —
1st ed.
    p. cm. — (FAQ: teen life)
ISBN-13: 978-1-4042-1973-1
ISBN-10: 1-4042-1973-0
1. Drug testing--Juvenile literature. I. Title.
HV5823.P66 2007
362.29'164—dc22

                                                    2006033524

Manufactured in the United States of America

Contents

Introduction

D o law enforcement and sports organizations have the right to test people for drug use? Does a school have the right to test its students for drugs? Questions like these have been the subject of intense discussion in the last decade or so. In 1995, the United States Supreme Court issued a decision in *Vernonia School District 47J v. Acton* that stated that schools do have a right to test athletes for the presence of drugs. The debate intensified in 2002, when the Supreme Court in *Board of Education v. Earls* narrowly ruled that it is lawful for schools to give random drug tests to students involved in other extracurricular activities, not only athletics.

The idea of regular drug testing is not new. It started in the early 1960s, when patients in drug treatment programs were required to submit urine tests. A few years later, the Olympic Committee banned the use of performance-enhancing drugs, requiring Olympic athletes to take drug tests. Around this time, the federal government also started administering drug tests to members of the armed forces serving in Vietnam. By 1986, consenting to drug tests became a requirement for all federal employees. Three years later, in two landmark cases, *Skinner v. Railway Labor Executives' Association* and *National Treasury Employees v. Van Raab*, the Supreme Court ruled that drug testing at work was constitutional when it protects the public's safety. By the mid-1980s, the practice was widespread in the

Failing a drug test can change someone's life forever. Tour de France winner Floyd Landis *(above)* claims his tests resulted in a false-positive reading. Whether Landis is right or not, his reputation is forever damaged.

private sector as well. Testing by employers spread, in part, because it is not specifically prohibited by the Constitution.

These antidrug measures in the workplace, like those enforced in schools, were met with vigorous opposition every step of the way. And they continue to be debated. Each side of the debate has a very convincing argument.

Arguments in Favor of Drug Testing

Most who support drug testing believe the public must be protected from the damage people can do while intoxicated. They argue that it is in the public interest to find out who is using drugs. Drug testing, in this scenario, is viewed as a tool for identifying those who are breaking the law and endangering themselves and others.

According to its supporters, drug testing is worthwhile because drug abuse is related to various well-documented problems in society. Policy reports issued by the Office of National Drug Control confirm this point: Compared to nonusers, illegal drug users were found to be sixteen times more likely to be arrested and booked for larceny or theft. Illegal drug users were also nine times more likely to be arrested and booked on assault charges. In addition, the U.S. General Accounting Office estimates that drug abuse costs the United States $110 billion a year. Much of these costs include lost productivity among workers and the burden of drug abuse on the nation's health care, legal, and penal systems.

Drug abuse is also a problem for social service agencies. It is the major factor in some of the more difficult social problems,

Police use drug tests and field sobriety tests to keep drunks off roads and highways. Four teens died in this wrecked car, which was driven by a drunk driver.

such as mental retardation from fetal alcohol syndrome, a birth defect caused by drinking alcohol while pregnant.

Moreover, alcohol and drug-related automobile crashes are the leading cause of death for high school students. And mass transportation and shipping accidents have occurred because a driver, pilot, or operator was under the influence.

Thus, because of concerns about on-the-job and customer safety, public health, crime reduction, and social welfare, supporters argue that drug testing should be done.

Arguments Against Drug Testing

Opponents of drug testing believe the practice is a violation of one of our cherished civil rights—the right to privacy. This right is provided by the Constitution. The Fourth Amendment, in particular, guarantees the right to freedom from unwarranted search. In other words, the right to privacy cannot be set aside without reason. It is illegal for the police to search your home, car, luggage, purse, clothing, or body without just cause. So what makes it acceptable for someone to "search" your blood or urine without a justifiable reason? Isn't that a greater violation of your right to privacy than someone's searching your pockets?

Drug testing can reveal facts that someone might want to keep private. For example, if you are taking medication for attention deficit disorder (ADD) or attention deficit hyperactivity disorder (ADHD), your sample may test positive for amphetamines. In that case, you would have to disclose your condition to whoever ordered the test. Otherwise, it may appear that you are taking amphetamines illegally. In the same way, if you take a legally prescribed medication for chronic pain, you may test positive for opiates in your system. This, too, would require disclosure of drug use.

Other opponents of drug testing argue that what they do at home, on their own time, is simply nobody's business. (Testing does not show when a drug was used, only that it was used at some time.)

Drug tests may also result in false positives—that is, they show drug use in someone who is not a user. This could ruin a person's

In 2002, Lindsay Earls *(right)* and her lawyer appeared in Washington, D.C. Their legal challenge to her school's drug testing policy went all the way to the U.S. Supreme Court.

reputation, wreck his or her chance to participate in athletic programs, and damage family trust. False positives have occurred when the person tested was using a cold or sinus medication or had eaten foods containing poppy seeds, among other reasons.

False negatives are possible as well. Someone may try to fool the test instead of trying to stop his or her drug habit. This raises the question of whether a particular drug-testing program would actually reduce drug use.

As you can see, there are arguments both for and against drug testing. The questions have more meaning when they are considered in real-life situations, especially when it comes to athletics and school, being stopped by the police, and employment.

Chapter one

WHAT ARE THE DIFFERENT TYPES OF DRUG TESTS?

It's important to know exactly what a drug test is and the different types of tests that are used. If you have ever been to the doctor for a checkup, you probably have been asked to give urine or blood specimens. When analyzed, these specimens give indications of your health. A doctor or nurse usually looks for, among other things, your blood sugar level (abnormal levels may indicate diabetes) and blood cell count (which reveal possible diseases such as anemia and leukemia).

Drug tests work in a similar way. Urine tests, hair tests, and blood tests are commonly used to determine if someone is using drugs. Broad-spectrum tests (also called polydrug screens) are another type. Some tests are better than others at identifying certain kinds of drugs, and some are more time sensitive than

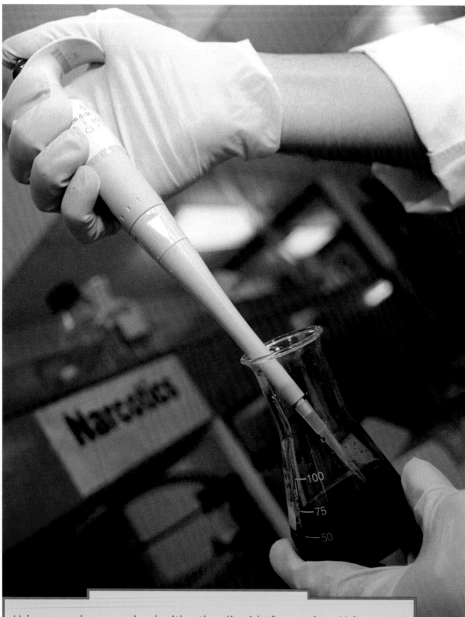

Urine samples are mixed with other liquids for testing. Urine tests like the one shown here are used to screen Olympic athletes for banned substances.

others. The National Institute on Drug Abuse (NIDA) tests for five types of drugs: methamphetamines, cocaine, opiates, marijuana, and PCP. These drugs, known as the NIDA 5, are part of a routine drug test.

Urine Tests

If you are to take a urine test, you will be given a plastic cup or test tube and asked to urinate in it in the bathroom. The container is then labeled with your name and sent to a laboratory where the actual test is performed.

Urine tests are of several types. Enzyme-multiplied immunoassay technique (EMIT) consists of observing whether or not special antibodies added to a urine sample react to show the presence of a particular drug.

Thin-layer chromatography (TLC) is a urine test that involves covering a glass slide with a thin layer of gel, then placing a single drop of urine on one end of the plate. Depending on what and how many drugs have been used, spots eventually appear in various places on the plate. Each one indicates the presence of a different substance.

Radioimmunoassay (RIA) is a test in which a radioactive substance is mixed with a urine sample. The substance seeks out particles of drugs, causing them to give off a level of radiation consistent with that particular drug. An instrument reads this signal and identifies what drugs, if any, are present in the sample. This test is extremely accurate, but somewhat expensive. It is used by the military.

Blood Tests

If you are asked to take a blood test, you can expect a doctor or nurse to insert a needle into a vein in your arm and draw a small vial of blood. This is a virtually painless procedure. The blood is analyzed for drugs in a laboratory.

Gas chromatography mass spectrometry (GCMS) is probably the most accurate of all the tests. A blood specimen is passed though a gaseous substance, which causes the molecules in the blood to separate. The molecules are then scattered onto a spectrometry screen according to weight. The result is a visual image that clearly identifies all substances in the sample.

GCMS has a nearly perfect record. It is wrong only once in a thousand trials, making it the test most widely accepted by the courts. The test is expensive, however, and relatively slow. In the event that the screening test is negative, the results are available within two or three days, depending on the lab. If further testing is needed, however, the results might not be available for five or six days.

Hair Tests

Testing of hair is becoming one of the most widely accepted methods of drug testing. It is considered less invasive than blood or urine tests. It also seems to be a better indicator of a wider range of drugs.

When someone uses a drug, the drug becomes a part of that person's body chemistry. Small quantities of the drug then become

Labs perform multiple tests on a single blood sample to reduce errors in their results.

Ten Great Questions to Ask Before Taking a Drug Test

1 Why am I being asked to take a drug test?

2 What kind of samples will be collected from me?

3 What drug(s) will I be tested for?

4 Which legal substances should I not take before a drug test?

5 Who will be informed of my drug test results?

6 Who can I withhold my results from?

7 What should I do if I test positive?

8 How do I contest a false positive result?

9 Can I use recent drug test results from my doctor instead?

10 What after-school activities will I be excluded from if I refuse to take a school drug test?

embedded in the protein of the hair. A one-and-a-half-inch-long sample of hair can provide a record of drug use for about ninety days. Longer samples can give a longer history of drug use, but environmental factors—shampoo, dye, or other chemicals—wear down the hair and reduce the drug concentration.

For a hair test, you will be asked to give a sample of hair about the thickness of a pencil and one and a half inches long. Usually, the sample is taken at the back of the neck. It first goes through a screening process and then may go through a more conclusive GCMS test to confirm the presence of a drug.

Sweat Tests

Sweat tests are a new form of drug testing. Drug courts and child protective services use weekly sweat tests to monitor individuals for evidence of substance abuse. A sweat patch is worn for seven to ten days, usually on the upper arm. To prevent tampering, it is designed in a way that shows if it has been taken off and reapplied. When the patch is removed for analysis, the perspiration collected on the patch is tested for the

This student has two swabs inserted in his mouth to obtain saliva samples for drug testing.

presence of drugs. If there's a positive result, a GCMS test is conducted on the perspiration sample for more specific and accurate results.

Saliva Tests

Saliva tests are becoming more commonplace because of their convenience and accuracy, which is said to be comparable to blood tests. Also, because a saliva sample is easy to obtain directly, it decreases the chances that a sample has been tampered with.

A swab is used to collect a saliva sample from inside the mouth. This sample can be analyzed in a lab for the presence of drugs using EMIT and GCMS tests. Also, there are some devices currently on the market that can produce results for drug courts and child protective services for the detection of methamphetamines, cocaine, opiates, and marijuana in ten minutes.

Broad-Spectrum Tests

These tests are so named because they identify a broad spectrum, or many different kinds, of drugs. They work by testing the environment, not by checking body fluids. The first broad-spectrum test was discovered by accident. The security company responsible for the trains that run in the tunnel under the English Channel from London to Paris has a detection device designed to check for the presence of explosives. The device can be programmed to detect drugs as well. The test, called IONSCAN, does have weaknesses: It does not detect alcohol, nor can it tell who is using a drug. It reveals only the possession of drugs. However, this information can be valuable in detecting drug dealers and smugglers.

Another broad-spectrum drug test is available for home use. Called DrugAlert, the test may be purchased for about twenty dollars. Parents seem to be the principal purchasers of the kit. Furniture, clothing, and other items are wiped with a chemically treated cloth, which picks up trace amounts of as many as thirty testable substances.

It is clear that drug testing is here to stay. The Supreme Court has ruled that it is constitutional to drug test federal workers and students who participate in sports and extracurricular activities. Additionally, while laws on drug testing vary in different states and municipalities, employers in the private sector can enforce drug testing policies for employees and job applicants. As a result, as many as fifty million drug tests are done annually in the United States.

Drug Detection Periods

How long drugs can be detected in the body depends on different factors, including how frequently a person uses a drug, what kind of drug is abused, and what kind of drug test is used. Some people believe there are hard and fast rules of drug testing or that there is a window of time in which they can temporarily stop using drugs in order to have a negative test. However, no waiting period can completely guarantee that a drug has completely left your system.

The chart on page 22 shows approximately how long drugs are detectable in the human body for the two more common tests: urine and hair tests. These are general time lines.

If you are interested in the results of a drug test, you can get yourself tested before your school or employer decides to. Some testing services supply confidential tests for hair or urine. You also can ask your doctor to give you a drug test. If you take different tests, however, you may get different results.

As tests become cheaper and easier to use, more parents are asking their teen children to submit to them. This may put you in an uncomfortable position. If you are abusing drugs, you are in a tight spot. If you are not abusing drugs, you may feel insulted

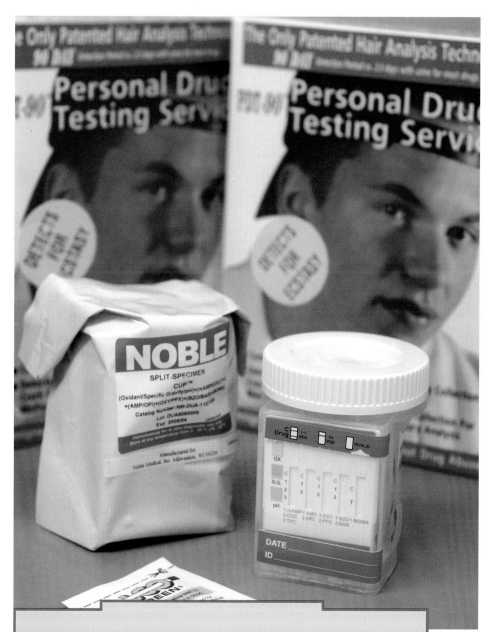

The home drug-testing kit shown here tests urine for the presence of ten common illegal drugs.

that your parents would suspect you of using them and you may want to refuse the test. In this case, the issue may have more to do with your relationship with your parents than with the question of your doing drugs. Instead of rejecting their request out of hand, use the opportunity to open up a discussion about communication and trust.

If you are in fact doing drugs, your parents are likely aware of it, and your problem with drug use is becoming more apparent or

Drug	Hair Detection Period	Urine Detection Period
Alcohol: beer, wine, liquor	Not Detectable	6–12 hours
Amphetamine/ methamphetamine (speed, crystal meth, ecstasy)	Up to 90 days	1–2 days
Barbiturates (pheno-barbital, secobarbital)	Unknown	2–12 days
Benzodiazepines (tranquilizers)	Unknown	1–42 days (longer period indicates heavy abuse)
Cocaine, crack	Up to 90 days	1–2 days
Opiates (codeine, morphine, heroin)	Up to 90 days	1–2 days
Marijuana (pot)	Up to 90 days	28–56 days

worsening. They are probably asking you to take a drug test as a chance for you to come clean and confront your problems. You would be better off admitting to substance abuse than letting your parents' suspicions and concerns escalate. Regardless of your particular situation, it is always best to be honest and open in these situations.

If you feel you can't talk to your parents, talk to a counselor, a coach, or an adult you can trust, or call a hot line. The important thing is to get your questions and feelings out in the open. If you are struggling with drug use, you need a support system. You can make the first move in helping yourself.

WHAT KIND OF DRUG TESTING HAPPENS IN ATHLETICS AND AT SCHOOL?

Sports is one area in which drug testing is done extensively. In many ways, drug testing owes its start to the field of athletics. Sports organizations test athletes for drugs because when an athlete uses drugs, his performance changes. Some drugs—anabolic steroids—can improve athletic performance. For example, the user can run faster or lift more weight. But in the long run, drugs hurt both the body and the mind. When someone competes using drugs rather than natural abilities, it is considered cheating.

Many organizations, such as the National Basketball Association (NBA) and National Hockey League (NHL), have a reasonable cause statement in their contracts with players. This means that the player agrees to drug testing if the owner has a good reason to believe that he or she has a drug problem.

Ben Johnson *(right)* saw his Olympic world record removed from the books after he tested positive for an illegal steroid.

Athletes and Steroids

Drug testing has changed the lives of many athletes. Some of them have had to leave sports forever because of a drug habit. Others have been able to turn their lives around.

Ben Johnson is a famous example of an athlete whose life was forever changed by a drug test. Johnson competed in the 100-meter dash in the 1988 Summer Olympics, representing Canada. When the race was over, Johnson had set a new world record at 9.79 seconds and had won the gold medal.

Soon after the race, however, Johnson tested positive for steroids. He was stripped of his gold medal, and the second-place finisher, Carl Lewis, was announced as the new gold medal winner. Johnson tested positive again, in 1993, and was banned from the Olympics for life.

The story of Ben Johnson sent a shock wave through the sports world. It showed that someone's drug use could become public knowledge—fast. It also showed how drugs can affect anyone. Johnson's steroid use couldn't have been proved without drug testing.

Athletes and Other Drugs

It may not surprise you that professional athletes use drugs recreationally. Professional sports figures have long had a reputation for being hard-hitting and hard-partying people. Especially in the past fifty years, professional athletes have earned celebrity status. Their large salaries put them in a unique position to experiment with drugs, but their fame makes it everybody's business when they have a drug problem.

In addition to testing for steroids, sports organizations also test for other commonly abused drugs, such as marijuana, cocaine, and amphetamines. The main reason for testing is that

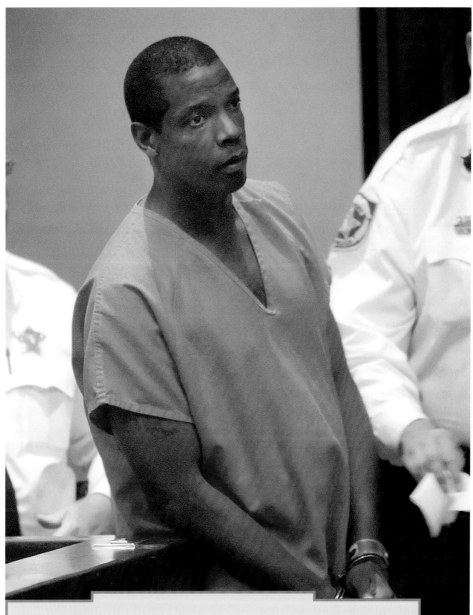

At nineteen, Dwight Gooden became the youngest All-Star in major league baseball history. By the time he was in his early forties, drug use had ruined his career and his life.

athletes' drug use may cost team owners a lot of money. Some players earn millions of dollars a year. That's a high price to pay for someone who won't be playing at peak ability. Owners need to protect such a large investment, and they consider drug testing a good way to do it. In these situations, testing is legal.

Drugs and Student Athletes

Because student athletes also face the pressure to perform at the top of their game, some may be tempted to take performance-enhancing drugs. Many high school athletes have hopes of receiving athletic scholarships and being recruited by college athletic teams, which could lead to a career as a professional athlete. It is estimated that between 6 and 11 percent of male high school athletes use steroids to bulk up and increase strength. Also, athletes of both sexes take stimulants, to enhance performance and fight fatigue, or diuretics, which help with weight loss.

The unfair advantages performance-enhancing drugs give athletes are well known, but the health risks of taking these drugs outweigh any win or championship. For instance, steroids pose unique dangers to teenagers whose bodies are still developing. They can cause damage to internal organs (especially the liver and heart), cause sterility, and even stunt growth. Stimulants can cause brain hemorrhaging and heart attacks. Using both types of drugs can have lethal consequences.

Urine and blood samples may be screened to detect the presence of steroids and performance-enhancing drugs. Student

Don Hooton *(above)* actively supports drug testing of high school athletes. His son used illegal steroids, became depressed, and committed suicide at age seventeen.

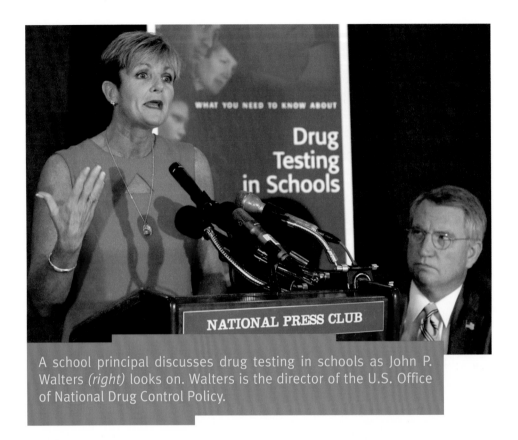

A school principal discusses drug testing in schools as John P. Walters *(right)* looks on. Walters is the director of the U.S. Office of National Drug Control Policy.

athletes may also be asked to submit samples to be tested for recreational drug use, as they must also comply with antidrug policies and consent to being screened for drug use. If you are an athlete and test positive for either performance-enhancing or recreational drug use, you may be thrown off the team.

The Acton Case

It is important for you to have information about drugs and what drugs can do to you. It is also important to know your legal rights when you are asked to take a drug test. Constitutional rights are your most basic rights. But those rights are affected by court decisions. The *Vernonia School District 47J v. Acton* case was important because it determined rights in the matter of drug testing in schools.

The Acton case began when James Acton, a seventh-grade student at Vernonia Elementary School in Oregon, signed up to play football. To allow him to play, James's parents had to sign a consent form for their son to be tested for drugs. However, his parents refused to sign the consent form, and the school refused to let James play after-school sports. The Actons sued, and the case eventually reached the U.S. Supreme Court.

The school administration had its own reason for starting a drug-testing program. They thought that testing was necessary because the school system had a problem. That was a very important part of the case. According to the administration, student athletes were using drugs and were attracted to the drug culture. The school tried many strategies to curb the problem, such as sponsoring drug awareness classes, providing counseling, and even suspending students. Nothing worked. The drug-testing program was supposed to help solve this problem.

When the Actons sued, a lengthy court process began. Finally the U.S. Supreme Court ruled that in this case drug testing was permissible. Because students are minors, they do not have the same right to privacy as adults. The dangers of drug use are so great that athletes must decide if they are willing give up their freedom from unwarranted search in order to participate in after-school sports programs.

Students Lindsay Earls and Daniel James sued their high school over its mandatory drug testing policy.

Beyond Sports: The Earls Case

School drug testing has become more widely accepted outside of the athletic arena. In 1999, the parents of Lindsay Earls, a high school student and National Honor Society member, sued the Board of Education of Tecumseh (Oklahoma) because of their policy of having students consent to a urine test if they wanted to participate in after-school activities. The *Board of Education v. Earls* case went all the way to the U.S. Supreme Court. In a close 5–4 decision, the Court ruled that the school board's policy was constitutional, stating that students participate in after-school activities on a voluntary basis and therefore agree to follow rules and meet requirements that do not apply to the rest of the student body.

If you test positive for drugs, the consequences are not relevant only to the policies of your school. Possession or use of illegal drugs is against the law. If you are found to possess illegal drugs, the police can arrest and jail you. Consuming alcohol if you are underage also is illegal.

Your school or athletic team may take immediate action against you as well. Many drug users are thrown off a team and excluded from school-related activities, such as school dances. They also face being expelled from school. If your drug test comes up positive, you will probably face similar consequences. Since drug testing is allowable at public schools at this time, you should be prepared for it.

Chapter three

WHAT SHOULD YOU KNOW ABOUT DRIVING AND DRUG TESTING?

If you are a young driver, it is crucial that you never get behind the wheel if you are impaired in any way by alcohol or drugs. Tragically, automobile accidents caused by drivers under the influence of alcohol and drugs are one of the leading causes of death among young people in the United States. The accidents are largely preventable, which makes alcohol and drug testing by the police a crucial part of keeping everyone on the road as safe as possible. Law enforcement officials use field sobriety tests that quickly reveal if a driver's ability to pay attention and process information is impaired. These tests are carried out at sobriety checkpoints and when someone is pulled over for driving recklessly.

Coordination Tests

Coordination tests help the police determine whether a person is impaired. One common test requires a person to

A police officer administers a coordination test at a sobriety checkpoint in San Francisco, California.

walk a straight line. In another test, the driver is asked to close his eyes, tilt his head, and touch his nose with his index finger. The driver may also be asked to stand on one foot for thirty seconds. People who are impaired have difficulties with these tasks. Coordination tests, however, do not identify the drug being used. Police officers often rely on the condition of a driver, observing speech patterns and odors emanating from breath or clothes, to help them determine if someone may be under the influence of alcohol or drugs.

Eye Observation Tests

Illicit drugs cause specific changes in the eyes and eyelids of users, which police are trained to look for. Eye observation tests are considered nonintrusive, because they do not require the consent of the person being tested. Eye symptoms that indicate drug use include red and watering eyes, droopy eyelids, slowly reacting, constricted, or dilated pupils, glassy eyes, or a blank stare.

Nystagmus eye tests are very specific and can be used as evidence in a court of law. The test involves holding an object, usually a pencil or finger, about twelve inches away from the person's face. Then the pencil or finger is moved toward him, around in circles, up and down, or from side to side. A person under the influence of alcohol or drugs will have involuntary jerky eye movements and will be unable to focus on the object for more than a few seconds. The signs are so obvious that these tests are considered reliable. However, they do not identify which drug the person is using.

Breath Tests

The best-known breath test is the Breathalyzer, used by police officers to determine whether someone, usually a driver, is impaired. The procedure is effective because alcohol in the blood system is present in exhaled breath. (About 5 percent of the alcohol is excreted by your lungs, and another 5 percent ends up in your urine. The majority is processed by the liver.) For a Breathalyzer test, the suspected drunk driver blows into a

A highway patrolman administers a Breathalyzer test. The driver was pulled over at a sobriety checkpoint.

Myths and Facts
About Drug Testing

Drinking cranberry juice or adding baking soda to a urine sample will help you pass a drug test.
Fact ➡ Cranberry juice, baking soda, and other home remedies cannot help you pass a drug test. Not using drugs is the only sure way of getting negative results.

Drug tests are only given to drug addicts.
Fact ➡ Being drug-free does not entirely exclude you from taking a drug test. In 2002, the U.S. Supreme Court ruled that schools can give random drug tests to students who want to participate in after-school activities.

Testing positive for drugs by an employer will get you fired. Fact ➡ Although testing positive for drugs may influence who hires you, it doesn't automatically get you fired. The American Disabilities Act protects workers who are recovering from substance abuse, or currently in treatment, from

discrimination. However, a positive drug test
result usually means the worker must get help.

tube connected to a container, which has a device for measuring
the amount of alcohol in the blood. It is highly accurate and is also
admissible in court. However, it measures only alcohol levels and
does not detect the presence of drugs in the body.

If You Test Positive

If you are found to be driving under the influence (DUI) or
driving while intoxicated (DWI), you have broken the law. A
police officer can place you under arrest, handcuff you, search
you for weapons, and jail you. (Your car will either be towed or
parked in a safe place.) You will need to post bail before you can
be released. Then you will most likely have to go to court.

There are very serious consequences if you test positive for
alcohol or drugs. And when an auto accident is involved, the laws
are even tougher. In all fifty states, it is illegal for drivers under
twenty-one years old to be driving after consuming any alcohol
at all. These zero-tolerance laws apply even if the blood-alcohol
concentration (BAC) reading is less than the amount needed for
adults to be considered legally impaired or intoxicated.

Conviction for DUI or DWI has many long-term consequences.
Your driver's license may be suspended, and you may have to
pay a fine and court fees. For a repeat offense, your car may be

This driver failed a roadside sobriety test. The police officer arrested him and will take him back to the station in handcuffs.

confiscated. Even if you regain your license, your car insurance rates will skyrocket. You may also be placed on DUI probation, which can last from three months to a year.

As a condition of DUI probation, some offenders are monitored to make sure they are not consuming any alcohol. New technology is being used to keep track of these offenders. Called a SCRAM unit (short for Sex Crimes Registration Apprehension and Monitoring unit), it similar to the electronic home monitors used for individuals under house arrest. The unit is worn on the ankle and detects alcohol from the surface of the skin. Every hour, it records a reading of blood-alcohol levels. At the end of the day, the SCRAM unit sends the results to a base unit, which is usually located in the probation office or court building. SCRAM units are becoming increasingly popular in the legal system because it is relatively easy to get around other ways of monitoring alcohol use.

IS THERE DRUG TESTING IN THE WORKPLACE?

Contrary to popular belief, drug users are not typically unemployed. In fact, one study estimated that as many as 71 percent of illegal drug users eighteen and older currently hold steady jobs.

Testing employees for drugs has become a $1.5 billion-a-year industry. Why is it the company's business whether or not its employees use drugs? The simple answer is that employees who use drugs are costly. Employee drug use has been linked to production problems, missed work, and accidental injuries, so companies have come to believe that drug testing makes good business sense. According to a study conducted by the Substance Abuse and Mental Health Services Administration, workers who did drugs had 250 percent more absences than those who didn't. In addition, the Occupational Safety and Health Administration

Drug-testing products make up a growing, multibillion-dollar market. Here, a product is on display at the annual conference of the Drug and Alcohol Testing Industry Association.

estimates that 65 percent of on-the-job accidents are related to substance abuse.

All of this adds dramatically to the cost of goods and services, which then increases the cost of all business products. The Department of Labor reports that substance abuse costs employers between 75 and 100 billion dollars a year—costs that are often passed on to consumers.

Reducing drug use means fewer accidents, higher production levels, fewer workdays missed, and more sales and profit. This means that drug testing at the workplace is a reality for a majority of the workforce. According to the American Management Association, 62 percent of employers had drug-testing programs in 2004.

Objections and Alternatives

The constitutionality of employee drug testing has been debated in the courts. The Supreme Court heard two cases in 1989 and, in both, the Court ruled that the practice is constitutional. In *Skinner v. Railway Labor Executives' Association* and in *National Treasury Employees v. Van Raab*, the Court decided that giving employees drug tests to protect public safety is a special priority and does not violate Fourth Amendment rights.

There have been objections to employee drug testing programs, however. For example, award-winning reporter and editor Valerie Harring refused to submit to drug testing by her employer, the *North Portland Sun-Herald* and was fired. She claimed that the paper was violating her civil rights and called drug testing "the witch hunt of the 1990s." Four other employees also quit.

Despite objections, companies continue to test. They tailor their programs to find what works best. Some companies place a just cause provision in their employee contracts. This means that the company will not test randomly but instead will test only employees who have given the employer a good reason to suspect them of drug abuse.

Because of a medical condition, this man was unable to supply his employer with a urine sample for testing. His letter of termination claimed that he "refused" to take the drug test.

All of the Home Depot's nearly 300,000 employees are subject to drug testing. The company says its policy protects customers and improves workplace safety.

Many options are available in cases of positive tests. Instead of firing, some companies let a person keep the job and undergo drug treatment. The employee is fired only if a second test is positive. Educational programs for employees and their families also increase the chances that they won't use drugs.

Federal Employment and Drug Testing

Drug testing has become a permanent part of federal employment. The government has a long history of involvement in the field of drug testing. This is true in several areas, especially in the military and in the Department of Transportation.

The military services began testing for drugs in 1970 as soldiers were returning from the Vietnam War. Because that program was successful, the various services began testing other personnel, starting an aggressive program of drug testing in the military. At present, the Department of Defense conducts about sixty thousand urine drug tests a month, as all personnel on active duty must be tested once a year.

At the U.S. Department of Transportation, drug-related accidents have underscored the need for drug testing. They also resulted in passage by Congress of legislation requiring alcohol as well as drug testing in 1991. People tested included mass transit workers, armed security personnel, signal maintainers, dispatchers, and vehicle operators. This policy currently affects about twelve million employees.

As it is in athletics and business, governmental drug testing has proved to be an effective means of reducing drug-related problems.

WHAT ARE YOUR LEGAL RIGHTS?

If you are asked to take a drug test, you are guaranteed certain rights.

The Right to Privacy

The right to privacy comes from a series of amendments to the Constitution. The Fourth Amendment, in particular, was written to protect civilians from having their homes and businesses searched without their consent (a common occurrence during the Revolutionary War). The right to privacy is now considered a fundamental right in the United States.

Protections Under the Right to Privacy

Several legal safeguards have been written to protect your right to privacy. These can apply to drug testing or

Shawn A. Heller *(center)* is the former director of Students for Sensible Drug Policy. He believes the current U.S. drug policy wrongly infringes on students' right to privacy.

10 FACTS ABOUT DRUG TESTING

1 A person's hair, blood, urine, saliva, and sweat can be tested for the presence of drugs.

2 Some illicit drugs can be detected in the body for a period up to ninety days.

3 Schools are allowed to test student athletes for drugs, as well as those who participate in extracurricular activities.

4 Drug tests usually screen for the presence of methamphetamines, cocaine, opiates, marijuana, and PCP.

5 Taking cold/sinus medicine or drinking ginseng tea can produce a false-positive drug test result.

6 According to the American Management Association, 62 percent of employers had drug-testing programs in 2004.

7 Drugs can be detected on surfaces and items such as furniture and clothing.

8 Fifty million drug tests are administered annually in the United States.

9 Field sobriety tests are used to check if a driver is under the influence of alcohol or drugs.

10 Informed consent guarantees your right to know when, why, and how a drug test will be given to you, as well as who will see your result.

in instances when you are asked to submit to any other physical search.

Probable Cause

Police officers may stop and question you for any reason. This might happen if they suspect that you are hiding something illegal or are otherwise breaking the law. You have the right not to answer their questions. But on the basis of your interaction, a police officer may determine whether or not to obtain a search warrant, which is a legal document stating that your property can be searched.

To get a search warrant, the police officer must go to a judicial official called a magistrate and ask for it. If the magistrate agrees that there is probable cause, a warrant will be issued.

Informed Consent

Informed consent is required if an officer wants to search you without having a search warrant. In other words, you must agree (give consent) to the search. Before you give your consent, you must be told exactly what the violation of privacy will be. This precaution applies to drug testing, too. The courts have ruled that your coach can't just hand you a specimen cup and say, "Urinate in this." He or she must tell you exactly what you are to be tested for.

If you are a minor and you are asked to take a drug test by an employer, make sure you have a consent form for your parents to review and complete before you allow any samples to be taken from you.

Imminent Danger

An officer may also act immediately if he or she feels someone's safety is in jeopardy. That means if someone is in imminent danger, or "clear and present danger." The courts have extended the meaning of "imminent danger" to cover random drug testing of workers such as airline pilots or bus drivers, who are entrusted with other people's personal safety. The Supreme Court has held that a clear and present danger to the public exists if someone in one of those jobs is impaired.

Procedures for Drug Testing

These procedures help ensure that the tests are performed correctly and done with your consent. If any of these procedures is not guaranteed, the results of your drug test may not be allowed as evidence in court.

This police officer was given consent by the tenant to search the apartment for drugs. In some situations, however, consent is not required to conduct a search.

Continuity of Evidence

Continuity of evidence means that there is a clear trail linking you to your drug test results. Every step of the drug test procedure must be clear. This guarantees that the specimen will not be tainted or mistaken for someone else's.

If you are taking a urine test, your specimen should be labeled immediately and then stored securely in a lab. The specimen must be tested by itself, with clean equipment. The results of the test must be written down immediately. If these precautions are not taken, you have a right to challenge the validity of the test results.

Confirming Tests

You have a right to ask for a confirming test, or second test. This is especially important if you believe that you had a false positive— failed a drug test when you were not using drugs. Don't hesitate to ask for a second test if you think the results are in error. Be sure to tell the evaluator about any medication you are using, both prescription and nonprescription. This is very important because, for example, Ritalin and certain over-the-counter drugs may produce a false positive for amphetamines.

Right of Refusal

In many cases, the courts have ruled that you have a right of refusal to any search done without a warrant. This means that you can refuse a drug test. This is true in a school setting. But if you don't take the test, you may have to suffer consequences, such as not being allowed to participate in after-school sports.

However, more is at stake if you refuse a drug test by the police—you can end up with a police record. The courts have ruled that refusing a police request to take a drug test is the same as an admission of guilt.

What the Future Holds

The answer to the question of what the future holds is clear. Drug testing will continue, and it may continue on more levels and with greater frequency. Drug testing also will become broader in scope. That is, more substances will be identified by a single test. Business, schools, and police are all looking for tests that will be easier to use and will identify more substances.

But what about the right to privacy? This issue continues to be debated. The Supreme Court has upheld the drug testing of employees, athletes, motorists, and students under certain circumstances. This means that, according to the courts, drug testing does not violate this important constitutional guarantee.

Yet you still need to know your rights in case you are tested. More important, you should know the consequences and dangers of using drugs. If you decide to be clean and sober, you are making a decision that will last a lifetime. Drug testing is not just about getting caught. It is about staying clean and reaching your potential.

Glossary

abuse Use of a drug in a manner other than that which is prescribed, especially a drug that is not medically indicated.

Breathalyzer Test that measures the amount of alcohol in the breath.

broad-spectrum test Test that identifies large numbers of drugs by testing the environment.

constitutional In agreement with the rights protected by the U.S. Constitution.

continuity of evidence Phrase meaning that a sample must be continually monitored to ensure that it came from a certain individual and has not been tampered with.

EMIT (enzyme-multiplied immunoassay technique) A common urine drug test.

eye observation test Test in which the eyes are observed for symptoms of drug use.

false negative Test result that wrongly identifies a person as a nondrug user.

false positive Test result that wrongly identifies a person as a user of drugs.

federal Relating to the central government.

fetal alcohol syndrome Birth defects caused by a mother's drinking while pregnant.

GCMS (gas chromatography mass spectrometry) A type of blood test.

informed consent Consenting to be searched by authorities with the knowledge of why, what, and how you will be searched.

IONSCAN Test that scans for persons transporting drugs.

just cause Phrase meaning that an official must have reason to suspect a person of using drugs before testing.

larceny The act of taking someone's property with the intent of keeping it.

magistrate A lower court judge or law officer.

methamphetamine Type of man-made drug that stimulates the nervous system.

nystagmus eye test Test of the eye's ability to focus and track.

opiate Drug derived from opium that depresses the nervous system.

PCP Phencyclidine, a drug once used to block pain during medical procedures by preventing certain signals from reaching the brain.

private sector Industries that are run by private owners (rather than by the government).

probable cause A reason authorities have to obtain a search warrant to search an individual's home and personal property.

right to privacy Constitutional right that guarantees that people will not have their privacy violated.

search warrant A legal document stating that a person's property can be searched to obtain evidence.

TLC (thin-layer chromatography) A common urine drug test.

Alcoholics Anonymous (AA)
Box 459, Grand Central Station
New York, NY 10163
(212) 870-3400
www.alcoholics-anonymous.org
  AA is a voluntary fellowship of people who share the
  goal of remaining alcohol free. In more than 150 countries,
  about two million members meet in 100,000 groups.

American Civil Liberties Union (ACLU)
125 Broad Street, 18th Floor
New York, NY 10004
www.aclu.org
  Founded in 1920, the ACLU is a nonprofit organization
  that aims to protect civil liberties, from the freedom of
  speech to the right to privacy.

Cocaine Anonymous (CA)
3740 Overland Avenue, Suite C
Los Angeles, CA 90034
(310) 559-5833
www.ca.org
  CA is a voluntary fellowship of men and women dedi-
  cated to abstaining from cocaine and drug abuse and
  providing a supportive environment for recovering
  drug users.

Narcotics Anonymous (NA)
P.O. Box 9999
Van Nuys, CA 91409
(818) 773-9999
www.na.org
An offshoot of Alcoholics Anonymous, NA states its mission as providing recovery and emotional support to drug users who desire a drug-free life. Currently, there are more than 33,500 weekly meetings in 116 countries.

National Alcohol and Substance Abuse Information Center (NASAIC)
(800) 784-6776
NASAIC's twenty-four-hour hotline offers information and advice on drug abuse.

National Council on Alcoholism and Drug Dependence (NCADD)
22 Cortlandt Street, Suite 801
New York, NY 10007-3128
(212) 269-7797
www.ncadd.org
Established in 1944, the NCADD seeks to educate the public on drug and alcohol abuse and provide help to those struggling with substance abuse issues.

National Institute on Drug Abuse (NIDA)
6001 Executive Boulevard, Room 5213
Bethesda, MD 20892-9561
(301) 443-1124
www.nida.nih.gov

As a part of the National Institutes of Health, NIDA aims to advance the understanding of drug abuse through science and research.

National Youth Crisis Hotline
(800) 442-4673 (HOPE)
This hotline offers around-the-clock assistance to teens who face crises, including drug abuse issues.

Web Sites
Due to the changing nature of Internet links, Rosen Publishing has developed an online list of Web sites related to the subject of this book. This site is updated regularly. Please use this link to access the list:

http://www.rosenlinks.com/faq/drte

For Further Reading

Aue, Pamela Willwerth. *Teen Drug Abuse* (Opposing Viewpoints). San Diego, CA: Greenhaven Press, 2006.

Minelli, Mark J. *Drug Abuse in Sports: A Student Course Manual.* Champaign, IL: Stipes Publishing, L.L.C, 2004.

Mur, Cindy. *Drug Testing* (At Issue). San Diego, CA: Greenhaven Press, 2006.

Newton, David E. *Drug Testing: An Issue for School, Sports, and Work* (Issues in Focus). Berkeley Heights, NJ: Enslow Publishers, 1999.

O'Hyde, Margaret, and John F. Setaro. *Drugs 101: An Overview for Teens.* Minneapolis, MN: Twenty-first Century Books, 2003.

Youngs, Bettie B., Tina Moreno, and Jennifer Leigh Youngs. *A Teen's Guide to Living Drug Free.* Deerfield Beach, FL: Health Communications, Inc., 2003.

Brown, Laura. "The Cost of Drug Testing Is Too High for
    Hawaii's Public Schools." *Hawaii Reporter.* February 19,
    2003. Retrieved July 25, 2006 (http://hawaiireporter.com/
    story.aspx?25420ecb-00c2-4a91-9420-411c1bd57178).

Coombs, Robert H., and Louis Joylon West, eds. *Drug Testing:
    Issues and Options.* New York, NY: Oxford University
    Press, 1991.

Holding, Reynolds. "Whatever Happened to Drug Testing?"
    Time.com. July 7, 2006. Retrieved July 28, 2006 (http://
    www.time.com/time/nation/article/0,8599,1211429,00.html).

Office of National Drug Control Policy. "Drug Related Crime."
    March 2000. Retrieved July 28, 2006 (http://www.
    whitehousedrugpolicy.gov/publications/factsht/crime/).

Schevitz, Tanya. "High School Students Debate Steroids
    Ethics." *San Francisco Chronicle*, p. B-1, December 7, 2004.

Index

Photo Credits